BUBBLE BUBBLE

BY MERCER MAYER

Parents' Magazine Press/New York

J
Easy
Mayer

Copyright © 1973 by Mercer Mayer
All rights reserved
Printed in the United States of America

Library of Congress Cataloging in Publication Data

Mayer, Mercer, 1943-
    Bubble bubble.

    SUMMARY: A little boy creates all sorts of
fantastic animals with his magic bubble maker.
    (1. Stories without words) I. Title.
PZ7.M462Bu   (E)   72-6167
ISBN 0-8193-0630-4   ISBN 0-8193-0631-2 (lib. bdg.)

For Laura, Leon and John Levin

MERCER MAYER, author and illustrator of many delightful picture books for children, was born in Arkansas and grew up in Hawaii. He studied at the Honolulu Academy of Arts and at the Art Students League in New York City. He has written and illustrated two other books for Parents' Magazine Press, **A Silly Story** and **Me and My Flying Machine** (the latter in collaboration with his wife Marianna). He has also illustrated **Boy, Was I Mad!** and **Goodbye, Kitchen,** both published by Parents.' Mr. and Mrs. Mayer make their home in the town of Seacliff on the North Shore of Long Island.